MVFOL

# My Middle Child, There's No One Like You

Dear Mama and Papa Bear:

Finally middle children get their very own book! I can hear middle children rejoicing all over the world—"It's about time!" Isn't it amazing how cubs from the same den can be so different? Chances are your middle cub is pretty much the opposite, personality wise, of the cub directly above him or her. Let's face it, parents, somehow the middle child feels squeezed between the firstborn prince or princess and the little schnooky bear.

The good news is that your middle child probably has lots of friends, enjoys competition, and is great at seeing both sides of an issue. And while the firstborn might excel in reading books, your middle child is most likely to be great at reading people. Guess what middle-born cubs grow up to become. Entrepreneurs. Bill Gates, Steve Forbes, and Donald Trump, to name a few, are all middle children. As a parent I'm sure you've discovered your middle child's qualities, such as loyalty, competitiveness, and the ability to be a great friend and a team player.

We wrote *My Middle Child, There's No One Like You* to celebrate the uniqueness of your middle child. You'll find the message in this book to be an encouragement to your middle child whether he or she is still a little cub or has already grown into adulthood. Give it as a gift or read it together to show him or her just how special he or she really is. Either way, we know you'll enjoy the book.

# My Middle Child, There's No One Like You

Dr. Kevin Leman
& Kevin Leman II

Illustrated by
Kevin Leman II

**Revell**
Grand Rapids, Michigan

Text © 2005 by Dr. Kevin Leman and Kevin Leman II
Illustrations © 2005 by Kevin Leman II

Published by Fleming H. Revell
a division of Baker Publishing Group
P.O. Box 6287, Grand Rapids, MI 49516-6287

Fifth printing, May 2006

Printed in the United States of America

Library of Congress Cataloging-in-Publication Data
Leman, Kevin.
    My middle child, there's no one like you / Kevin Leman and Kevin Leman II; illustrated by Kevin Leman II.
        p.   cm.
    Summary: Mama Bear describes to her middle-born cub all the qualities that make her special.
    ISBN 10: 0-8007-1830-5
    ISBN 978-0-8007-1830-5
    [1. Bears—Fiction. 2. Middle-born children—Fiction. 3. Birth order—Fiction. 4. Mother and child—Fiction.] I. Leman, Kevin, II, ill. II. Title.
PZ7.L537345My 2005
[Fic]—dc22                                              2004024213

For my two older sisters, Holly and Krissy.
You're my favorites. I love you.
—Kevin Leman II

Three little cubs come
out of the same den, and,
oh my, are they different!

irst is the worst, second is the best, third is the nerd with the hairiest chest!" The middle-born bear cub ran into the den, all out of breath.

"My, my, Middle Cub!" Mama Bear said. "What was that all about?"

"She said you loved her the best! But I told her that's not true. It isn't, is it? Who do you love the best, Mama?"

"She shouldn't have teased you like that," Mama Bear said as she scooped Middle Cub right up into her lap. "But that's okay. Because I have a surprise for you!"

Mama Bear grabbed her photo album and opened it up. Then she nuzzled her nose down close to Middle Cub's ear so the other cubs couldn't hear and said, "Let's see . . ."

We were anxious to meet
you right from the start!

ama Bear opened to the first page. "We were a very happy family. But we still wanted another cub. The day we found out you were on your way, we were so excited! Papa Bear gave high fives to anyone who would lift a paw! He pulled out the changing table, and he dusted off the diaper bag. Since you weren't our first cub, things didn't seem so scary this time around. We knew what to expect."

"Was I just like you thought I'd be?"

"Well, not exactly."

When the doctor laid you across my lap, I was so happy I cried. I knew right then that you were a unique gift from God. You were your own special cub. And do you know what I discovered?"

"What, Mama?"

"You were nothing like I expected. I never thought my cubs could come out of the same den and be so different. But right from the beginning, everything about you was almost the very opposite of Firstborn Cub."

"Really? How?"

"Well, with Firstborn Cub, I had to go to the hospital as soon as the rooster crowed, but you decided to arrive in the middle of the night!"

Middle Cub nodded. "I've always been a night-owl bear. Does that mean you love me the best?"

Mama Bear smiled and turned the page.

Your special day
started in the middle
of the night!

You adored your
baby brother . . .
sometimes.

Right from the start, you were a pleasure to be around, a one-of-a-kind cub. And even though you wore hand-me-downs and played with your older cubling's toys, you were always your very own little bear. You rolled with the punches—even when it was your little brother bear throwing them!"

Middle Cub laughed out loud at that. "What else, Mama? Tell me more!"

"Well," Mama Bear continued, "you have a talent for understanding others and for caring about them. Remember when I brought Baby Bear home for the first time? You treated him like he was a living teddy bear. You immediately shared your toys with him, and you always gave him a little hug before you went out the door to school."

"I didn't like to leave the den, did I, Mama?"

"Well, let's see . . ."

There you are—surrounded
by your many friends
at school!

When you first went to school, you were pretty scared, but your older cubling sat you down and told you all about the fun things you'd do in Ms. Skunkster's class. It was nice that your sister could show you the way, wasn't it?"

Middle Bear nodded happily.

"You looked up to her as the big bear on campus. And even though you had the same teachers and the same classes, you acted very differently in school."

"What do you mean, Mama? Did I get better grades?"

"That's not what I mean, sweetie. Your sister read lots of books, but you seemed to read other cubs. You made friends so easily. Today when the phone rings or there's a knock on the den door, we know it's for you."

"If I had so many friends, why is there only one picture of me with them?"

"Well, let's see . . ."

Even on your birthday, those two moved in on your turf.

ou know, honey, it was hard keeping up with you little cubs all the time. You kept us so busy, it wasn't easy to remember to buy film or charge up the video camera batteries. But I cherish the eleven pictures I have of you, sweetie. And you held your own with the others in those pictures."

Middle Cub grinned. "It wasn't easy with them always poking their heads in, hogging up my photos."

"That's what I love about you. Even though I'm sure you felt squeezed between the other cubs or lost in the shuffle, you never let it bother you."

"That's why you love me the best?"

"Well, let's see . . ."

With you there is so much to love!" Mama Bear said. "Did you know that you're a peacemaker?"

"Is that the thing they put in Grandpa Grizzly's chest to make his heart work better?"

"No, honey, that's a pacemaker. A peacemaker is somebody who keeps things calm between those who tend to fight. When your cublings tease each other and you're in the middle, you keep your cool and don't make the situation worse. Papa and I notice that. You set such a good example for your younger cubling."

"How else am I a peacemaker, Mama?"

"Well, let's see . . ."

Fair-N-Square Bear

Our little peacemaker was blessed with good judgment and common sense!

No bear could pull off ugly
as cute as you could!

Do you remember the stage shows Firstborn Cub would direct?"

Middle Cub giggled. "Those were fun! But I always had to be the bad bear."

"That's right. Firstborn Cub could be a little bossy, and she always got to be the princess. But you were the best bad bear you could be. You never quit just because you didn't get your way." Mama Bear thought for a minute. "You didn't have the spotlight, but you were never in the shadow."

"So you love me the best because I'm always a peace-maker?"

"Well, let's see . . ."

I never said *always*. You have a wild hair sometimes, you know. There was a time when you would do the opposite of whatever Papa Bear or I wanted you to do. So we reminded you how special you are to us. We were lucky that phase didn't last long."

"I'm sorry."

"Oh, don't be sorry. It's part of growing up. You had to remind us that you were different from Firstborn Cub and that we needed to treat you differently. So we started dressing you in different clothes, and we put you on a soccer team, something your sister never tried. We even made sure you had your own special traditions at Christmas."

"You did all that just for me? I really must be your favorite!"

"Well, let's see . . ."

You found your place
in the world with a
kind heart and fancy
footwork!

You were content to
let your sister lead,
even on Christmas
morning!

W hat part of Christmas do you love the best?" Mama Bear asked.

"I like getting presents, but I love giving them too."

"That's right. You love to make your family happy. Even when you were a tiny bear, we could see that any gift we gave you was fine with you. As long as you could be close to your family at Christmas, you were content."

"I'll bet I can spell *content*—even though it's a hard word!"

"Well, let's see . . ."

Content. C-O-N-T-E-N-T," Middle Cub spelled. "Now do you love me the best? Because I'm the smartest cub?"

"Well, that does remind me of all the contests you created: the Singing Showdowns, the Dancing Duos, Surviving the Snails . . . You sang and danced, held your breath, and twirled your baton with all your heart. Sometimes Firstborn Cub would have the upper paw because she was older. But when you won, you let everyone know it! 'The underdog bear won!' you'd shout." Mama Bear smiled. "But there's one contest where nobody can beat you."

"What's that, Mama?"

"Well, let's see . . ."

26

With seven slippery snails, our **competitive cub** wins—paws **down**!

Mama Bear shares her favorite
sandwich and a special secret.

Mama Bear thought for a moment. Then her eyes lit up. "What's your favorite sandwich?"

"That's easy—raspberries and honey!"

"That's my favorite too. And you know what? In our family, you're the honey. You're the sticky part in the middle that holds us together. You're the best part."

"The best part?"

"I fell in love with you the day you were born. You are my special cub who makes my heart smile. You'll always be a part of me, and I'll always be a part of you. There's no one like you, my happy little middle cub, and I love you."

"I love you too, Mama. I'm going to stay here with you forever, right?"

"Well, let's see . . ."

Middle Cub may have been
squeezed in the center
all those years, but looking
back, there's no place
she'd rather be!